No Room for Dessert

Also by Hallie Durand
Dessert First
Just Desserts

No Room for Dessert

by Hallie Durand

with illustrations
by Christine Davenier

atheneum books for young readers

NEW YORK   LONDON   TORONTO   SYDNEY   NEW DELHI

ATHENEUM BOOKS FOR YOUNG READERS
An imprint of Simon & Schuster Children's Publishing Division
1230 Avenue of the Americas, New York, New York 10020

This book is a work of fiction. Any references to historical events, real people, or real locales are used fictitiously. Other names, characters, places, and incidents are products of the author's imagination, and any resemblance to actual events or locales or persons, living or dead, is entirely coincidental.

ATHENEUM BOOKS FOR YOUNG READERS is a registered trademark of Simon & Schuster, Inc.

For information about special discounts for bulk purchases, please contact Simon & Schuster Special Sales at 1-866-506-1949 or business@simonandschuster.com.

The Simon & Schuster Speakers Bureau can bring authors to your live event. For more information or to book an event, contact the Simon & Schuster Speakers Bureau at 1-866-248-3049 or visit our website at www.simonspeakers.com.

Also available in an Atheneum Books for Young Readers hardcover edition

Book design by Lauren Rille
The text for this book is set in Adobe Garamond Pro.
The illustrations for this book are rendered in pen and ink washes.
Manufactured in the United States of America
0512 OFF
First Atheneum Books for Young Readers paperback edition
June 2012
10 9 8 7 6 5 4 3 2 1
The Library of Congress has cataloged the hardcover edition as follows:
Durand, Hallie.
No room for Dessert / Hallie Durand; illustrated by Christine Davenier. — 1st ed.
p. cm.
Summary: Eight-year-old Donahue "Dessert" Schneider is feeling completely ignored and unloved at home, but she is certain that will change when her invention wins the Thomas Edison Contest at school.
ISBN 978-1-4424-0360-4
[1. Family life—Fiction. 2. Inventions—Fiction. 3. Schools—Fiction. 4. Brothers and sisters—Fiction. 5. Restaurants—Fiction.]
I. Davenier, Christine, ill. II. Title.
PZ7.D9313No 2011
[Fic]—dc22   2010022039
ISBN 978-1-4424-0361-1 (pbk)

For Gabrielle and Donald McGhee,
my parents—I love you
—H. D.

CHAPTER ONE

NOT QUITE ENOUGH

It says in my baby book that when I was born, my parents couldn't believe how big and beautiful I was—I weighed nine pounds and five ounces, and I'm convinced that's why they called me Donahue Penelope Schneider—they wanted a fancy name to match my size. That tells you how important my arrival on this planet was to them. It also says in my baby book (I read it a lot) that when I was born, the weather was warm, sunny, and welcoming, and the trees were just beginning to bloom. And that's not all—it says I was the best baby ever, my head was perfectly shaped and my eyes were navy blue, my fingers were long, I smiled before I was six weeks old, and I rolled over at three months! My grandmother even gave me a special nickname, "Dessert," because I was the sweet treat she'd secretly been hoping for (her first grandchild). And I've always signed my name like this to let the world know how I feel about myself:

Dessert

But it's not like that anymore. I'm eight now, my grandmother went on two years ago,

I'm in third grade, and I'd bet you fifty bucks that my parents don't even know whether I'm learning fractions, multiplication, or my ABCs this year. They probably don't even know how many teeth I've lost so far. That's the truth.

This morning I was reminded that I'm nobody these days. It was Saturday, and I was late to breakfast because I wanted to braid my hair. I don't usually do stuff with my hair, but I didn't want Mummy to see how dirty it was. We have crepes on Saturdays before my parents go to our restaurant, Fondue Paris (you can probably guess we serve fondue there). Dad is the chef, and Mummy is "front of house." That means she has to smile at the customers, even on days when she'd rather not.

I divided my hair into three sections and began to make my braids. Just as I got going, I heard a sizzling noise downstairs, and I smelled butter. Dad must have poured the batter into the frying pan. Crepes (they should be spelled k-r-e-p-s) look like the skinniest pancakes you've ever seen. We get to pick our own toppings, too. That's my job, and I like to line them up so they look like they're for sale in a grocery store.

I always put honey in the lineup as a courtesy because everybody likes it but me—

I don't think it's much better than mayonnaise. Then comes the red jam (without seeds), marmalade, Nutella (which I love because it tastes like chocolate perfume), smoked ham (my dog Chunky's favorite), brown-yellow mustard, and peanut butter, which Mummy says is the "Queen" of them all.

I finished my braids and ran downstairs. But when I got to the kitchen, I saw right away that something was wrong. The toppings were all mixed up around the table, and everybody was eating without me—I doubt they would have noticed if I hadn't shown up at

5

all. First there was my four-year-old sister, Charlie, who looked like her face was attached to her plate.

Then on the other side of the table were the Beasties, my brothers, Wolfie and Mushy—Wolfie's two, and he already had Nutella all over his hands, and Mushy's one, and there was red jam everywhere. Mummy and Daddy looked like they were in a race to see who could finish eating first (they always talk about good manners, but privately they're speed-eaters).

Just as I was about to sit down, Mushy pointed at my head and said, with a capital "D" at the beginning and a perfect "T" at the end, "DIRT."

Mummy and Daddy started clapping.

"Mushy knows your name!" Mummy exclaimed.

"My name's not DIRT," I said.

"DIRT," said Mushy.

"It's close enough," said Mummy.

"Is not," I said, but she didn't even turn her head. So I reached for the Nutella, but when I took the lid off, it was nearly empty. I needed a rubber scraper. Why had I even bothered to cover up my dirty hair? Mummy wouldn't notice if I never washed it again in my entire life. And how could she possibly think "Dirt" was "close enough" to my name? Worse, it wasn't even nine o'clock in the morning yet. . . . There was plenty of time for more rotten stuff to happen today. . . .

CHAPTER TWO

FOSTER BROOKS

The following Tuesday, three desks over from mine at school, I saw somebody I didn't recognize. He had on an orange shirt. His hair was sort of a mess, and I thought he might have bed head like Wolfie, or else it was just wavy. I could only see his eyes a little from the side, but I'm pretty sure he was squinting. Did he need glasses? Mummy doesn't like it when I stare at people, so I held my hand up to the side of my face and looked at him through my fingers. Now he was pulling his eyelashes.

Then our teacher, Mrs. Howdy Doody, stood up like a big sunflower and said, "My dear happy learners, today is brand-new, in all kinds of ways!" I was still watching the new boy through my fingers, and I saw him look up when Mrs. Howdy Doody said that. She looked right at him and said, "Our third-grade family has a new member! Please welcome Foster Brooks to Lambert Elementary."

Now I knew what to call him. I liked the name Foster Brooks because it sounded like a movie star. He looked a little bit like a movie star too. But when we all started clapping to welcome him, he put his head down and waved his arms above him as if his car had broken down on the highway. Did he mean

"get lost" or "help"? I could still see
the side of his face, and it was turning a little red—I thought it might
be the kind of red that meant he
didn't want to be in our class.
That would make sense if he
was trying to say "get lost."
But it could be that he
didn't want Mrs. Howdy
Doody calling attention to
him when his hair was such
a mess. Especially because
when she says your name
in front of the whole class,
you get forty-two eyeballs on
you. . . . That's like being

on stage. So I decided to take my own eyeballs off him and put my hand back up—looking through my fingers seemed nicer than a full-on stare.

He did a lot of things. He picked up his pencil and put it back down (was he inspecting it?), he scratched his ear (probably itchy), and then he played with his eyelashes again (my guess was he had crummies in his eyes). Next he brushed the eyelashes off his desk (that told me he was tidy), stared at his thumbs (bet he likes thumb wars), moved his chair a tiny bit closer to me, erased something (more evidence he was tidy), matted down the back of his hair with his hand (that convinced me it *was* bed head), sneezed into his elbow (Mrs. Howdy Doody would love that!), looked under his chair, nodded to Mrs. Howdy Doody when she came over and whispered something to him, shook his head, nodded again, and wrote something on a piece of paper. Wow. Now I understood why Mrs. Howdy Doody always says, "Watch and learn."

I kept my fingers up and tried to see what he was writing. He was too far away. I tried to get my eyes a little closer, but this time he was looking right back at me, and he was making scissors with his hand.

He was telling me to cut it out. Crud. He made some more "cuts" at me, and then turned

his head away. And even though he hadn't spoken out loud yet, I knew two things about Foster Brooks. He didn't like being stared at, and he was probably good at charades.

CHAPTER THREE

A SILVER NOTEBOOK

The very next day I felt like Mrs. Howdy Doody must have been watching a reality show about my life, because the first thing she said was, "How many of you would like to make your lives easier?" We all raised our hands. Mrs. Howdy Doody raised her hand too, and then she said, "My life would be easier if I had a chauffeur to drive me around! Why, just this morning, when I had to back in between two other cars in the faculty parking lot, I realized that driving backward is *not* my specialty. . . . And since I don't have a chauffeur, I thought how much easier my life would be if I had a driver's seat and steering wheel facing out the *back* of the car as well as the front. I'd never have to drive in reverse!"

Mrs. Howdy Doody put her arms out as if they were holding a steering wheel and walked toward us. She said, "There was once a great inventor, who brought the world light. His mission was to improve people's lives." (I paid good attention now because I liked the sound of this man.) She "drove" left and said, "His name was Thomas Edison."

She "drove" forward a few steps and said, "Thomas Edison invented long-burning light-bulbs, and the phonograph, and the first movies, too!" I definitely knew about the light-bulb, but I didn't know about the movies. . . .

Mrs. Howdy Doody "drove" really fast straight across the room and said, "And now it's time for you to be visionaries! It's time for *you* to invent!" Without going backward, Mrs. Howdy Doody made a few more turns and ended up back at her desk.

Then she announced that our Invention Unit would not be a "unit" at all. She said we would learn about inventing in the form of a contest, the Thomas Edison Contest. And we were *all* supposed to come up with inventions to improve our lives. That didn't sound very hard, and I thought a contest sounded better than homework because somebody was going to win. Since there are only twenty-one kids in our class, I had a pretty good chance!

"Thomas Edison filled three thousand five hundred notebooks with his ideas!" said Mrs. Howdy Doody. She patted the top of a big stack of silver notebooks that was sitting on her desk. "We'll start the contest by writing down our invention ideas," she continued as she handed us each a notebook. "For the rest of the week, we'll fill our notebooks with ideas to make our lives better, just like Thomas Edison did.

"Let your minds dance!

"Let your minds go crazy!

"Let your minds fly to the moon and back!"

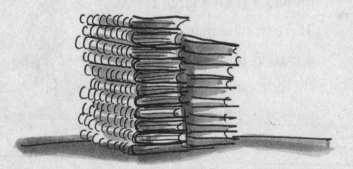

If ever there was a contest I might be able to win, this was it, because I'm a visionary. I got it from my dad. He invented the Eiffel

Fondue Tower at our restaurant. You probably don't know what it is unless you've been there. The tower is as high as a basketball hoop, and at the bottom, in the middle, is a giant silver fondue pot (it's a lot wider than a large pizza). There's a tube that looks like a garden hose coming out the side, and every day it pumps a different flavor of sweet, delicious dessert fondue all the way up to the top.

Then the fondue comes streaming back down

Fondue Paris
TAKE YOUR FLIGHT TONIGHT

through the middle, like water coming out of a faucet. You get to take your bowl right up to the tower and hold it under the stream until it's all the way full. Dad says our customers worship the Fondue Tower, and I worship it, too. There were at least one hundred pages inside my notebook, and I just hoped my pencil could keep up with my brain, which felt like it was going about a hundred miles per hour!

My first idea came easily—a machine to read people's minds. If I had one, I would know everything I wanted to know about Foster Brooks. It could be kind of like having a Magic Eight Ball inside my head. I could ask it, *Does Foster Brooks have a pet?* And it would say back yes or no. I could ask if

Amy D. would be in my class next year, and if it said yes, I could plan ahead. (Amy D. does not have a nice bone in her whole body, and she thinks she's cool because she shows horses and her dad has a radio talk show.) I'd also know what Evan was writing down in his notebook. I'd be able to see how he fits all the stuff he knows in his head, too. It's about the same size as the rest of ours, but there's way more in it.

CHAPTER FOUR

THE FRIDGE

My stomach was growling when I got home, so I marched straight into the kitchen and let my backpack drop to the floor. But I stopped before I opened the fridge. Something was different. It didn't take me too long to figure out what it was. I couldn't see my school picture anymore. Instead, I saw a brand-new work of art by Wolfie. It took up most of the fridge. There were four plastic flowers stuck on the front, one orange, one green, and two magenta, and a bunch of small, yellow, plastic duck stickers. There was a silver-blue turkey with a long neck, too, but half of it was not even on the page. Wolfie couldn't even put a sticker on right. He had not drawn one thing on this picture himself. All he had done was stick some ugly stuff on a piece of paper—a very big piece of paper.

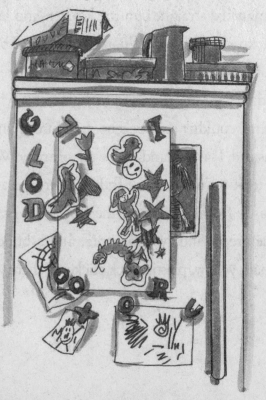

And somebody in our house must have thought it was good enough to cover my school picture. I had a feeling that somebody was one of my parents. On closer inspection, I noticed that there were plenty of things that had *not* been covered by Wolfie's masterpiece—a thank-you note to Mummy from her sister, two magnets from Charlie's preschool, and Mushy's birth announcement—that was more than a year ago already. I couldn't see a single thing of mine on there . . . anymore.

Mummy came in with some groceries and told me to get the rest out of the car. "You covered my school picture," I said.

"Just bring in the bags," Mummy said

back. "I've got to get your brothers." I knew what this meant. That Mummy thought unbuckling the Beasties' car seats was more important than my school picture. It meant that she thought it was perfectly fair to carry Wolfie, who was capable of walking himself, while I carried the groceries. To make it worse, I didn't even get to go grocery shopping. Mummy knows I like grocery stores. She knows I like to see the new things they have, and that I'm also still light enough to ride on the back of the cart. Sometimes I even push an extra cart for her, because hers is always full of the Beasties. I noticed that Charlie snuck right inside without carrying a thing. Mummy didn't make her help at all.

It was just another reminder that Wolfie is Mummy's favorite after Mushy, but that she still likes Charlie better than me.

I brought in the bags and went up to my room to play with my china dogs. My dogs can do a lot, but I can't bend them because they're china. And that's when I thought of making china dogs with opposable thumbs. That would be a great invention. I jotted it down in my notebook. They'd be able to do so much more if they could bend their thumbs. We played together the rest of the afternoon until Mummy said it was supper-time. Once my dogs were safely tucked back in their crate, I went to the kitchen, and the Eat-It-Up Fudge Pudding sitting on my plate was still steaming. Things were looking up, until I checked around the table and saw right away that I had the smallest portion. In the old days I would have thought this was an accident, but not today. I'm smarter now.

"Mine's the smallest," I said.

"They're all the same," said Mummy. But I knew they were not all the same. All I had to do was look around the table to see that I'd been gypped. And that's when I wished there was a scale in my plate like they have when you check out at the grocery store. I'd have to remember to write that down.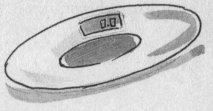

"Mushy has more than I do," I said a little louder. But Mummy didn't seem to hear me. Mushy's face was already covered with fudge sauce, and Wolfie was attacking his half-baked brownie pieces. Charlie hadn't picked her head up the whole time—as usual, she wanted the trip from her

29

plate to her mouth to be as short as possible. And even though it wasn't all that long ago that I fought and won the battle to eat dessert before supper for the whole family, it seemed like prehistoric times.

CHAPTER FIVE

A PRODIGIOUS NOTE TAKER

I had reason to make another note before I went to bed. Chunky and I sleep side by side, and even though my bed's not queen-size, we fit in just fine. The only problem is that he already has a blanket (his fur), and I don't. That made me think of my next invention, a blanket-suit you plug in. It would look like my fuzzy feety pajamas, but it would be electric! We wouldn't need a blanket at all. I wouldn't get too cold, and Chunky wouldn't get too hot. I wrote "Plug-In Fuzzies" in my silver notebook. I had definitely inherited Dad's visionary brain cells.

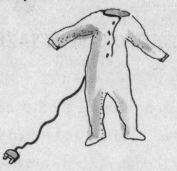

And my visionary brain cells must have multiplied overnight. Because as soon as the Beasties started rattling their cribs the next morning, I thought, *If I didn't have to hear that rattling, my life would be much better.* I realized that the Beasties' crib bars could work just like Chunky's invisible fence. Each of the Beasties would wear a collar, and if they touched their crib bars, they would get a little shock, enough to keep them from touching the bars again, exactly the same way Chunky's system works. It might take the Beasties longer to learn to stop rattling the bars than it took Chunky to learn to stay in our yard, but I knew it would work.

With my Collar-&-Crib System, my brothers would never wake me up again!

My visionary brain cells were busier than I ever could have imagined. New ideas came to me everywhere I looked. When I heard Charlie waking up, I thought about how long it takes her to choose her clothes. And voilà! I had another invention—an Automatic Dresser. All you'd have to do is enter some simple data about the weather and where you were going. There could be choices like school, gym, biking, playground, and church. Once you entered the information, a drawer would open with an outfit inside it. The other drawers would stay locked. The dresser would make the choice for you! Then I wouldn't have to hear

Charlie screaming about what to wear. I had thought of three ideas since supper last night—Plug-In Fuzzies, Collar-&-Crib System, and the Automatic Dresser, and all three of them involved electricity—imagine what Thomas Edison would think about this if he were here to witness it. Inventing was a piece o' cake!

I always sit with Sharon S. and Bonnie A. on the bus (behind Evan C.). Sharon had plans

for a tiny washing machine for doll clothes. She had even drawn a picture to go with her idea, and it looked like a salad spinner.

It was really good. And Bonnie had two ideas so far. One was Marshmallow Milk, which you could make in a blender. I wondered if it might be too sticky. Her other invention was a Stretchy Arm, so she could reach across the table and steal her sister's food or pick up her room without moving. It sounded really useful, and it would probably be popular. Evan was working on a Flying Car. This had something to do with repelling magnets, but the way he explained it was so boring, it hurt my brain.

At school Mrs. Howdy Doody asked how many of us had already written down some ideas, and everybody raised their hand. "You're prodigious note takers!" Mrs. Howdy Doody said. "Just like Mr. Edison. You're taking a lot of notes!" Then she held up a picture she'd drawn of her Reversible Car. It had an extra row of seats in the back, where the rear-facing steering wheel was. "You can draw diagrams, too." I thought about Sharon's Doll-Clothes Washer and the cute picture she'd already made. She deserved extra credit today.

"Just remember!" said Mrs. Howdy Doody. "Whether you draw, write, or do something in between—Mr. Edison proved that from quantity comes quality, so go ahead and be prodigious. Go ahead and fill your notebooks!"

CHAPTER SIX

A CONVERTIBLE LAP SEAT

The quality of my inventions was high, and I probably had the most already, too. Thomas Edison would be amazed that I had both quality and quantity. And what happened to my brain after school is proof that my visionary brain cells had done a lot more than multiply—they had moved right in and planned to stay for a while!

Let me explain. When I came home, there was a stack of books on the coffee table, and Charlie was asking Mummy to read one.

Mummy said okay, and even though I don't think she's read to me since the last solar eclipse, I was curious about what book Charlie chose. So I went into the living room, but I couldn't even see Charlie's book because she and the Beasties were all fighting over Mummy's lap. Charlie was pushing Wolfie and Mushy off one leg, and then as soon as she got in the middle, Wolfie and Mushy pushed her back off the other leg. It didn't take Mummy very long to say, "ENOUGH." What happened next didn't surprise me, and it won't surprise you, either. She placed Mushy right in the middle of her lap. Then she assigned Charlie to the right and Wolfie to the left, and she told them that if they made another sound, she would stop reading, and if they didn't believe her, they should just try it.

That's when I opened my backpack, got out my silver notebook, and wrote down "Lap Seat." It would look like a seesaw, but it wouldn't be as long. It could be laid across Mummy's lap, and the three of them could sit together on it. I'd put Charlie closer to the middle because she weighs more. I made a quick sketch. Then, as I went upstairs, I had another incredible idea. The Lap Seat could be converted into a slide for playtime. And you could use it on the stairs. That would be more the kind of game we'd get to play when Pam was babysitting, but still, I felt really good about the idea. I called it the Convertible Lap Seat.

My inventing skills were getting better and better—this was the first time I had started with one idea and it had become a double idea. In less than a minute, my simple Lap Seat had become a Convertible Lap Seat. My mind was on fire! There was no way anybody else's brain cells would be able to keep up with mine. I wondered what the prize for the contest was going to be.

Mummy served us each a Mallomar before our spaghetti pie that evening. Normally I would have been happy because Mallomars are store-bought cookies, which means they are exactly the same size. Each one is a little marshmallow mound that sits on top of a graham-cracker platform. The whole thing is dunked in dark chocolate. If you stretch your mouth, you can fit the entire Mallomar in at once. (That's what I do.) But the Mallomar didn't taste that good to me tonight, because I knew that Mummy must have bought them for the Beasties when they all went grocery shopping without me. Mushy probably just pointed at them from the cart, and the next thing he knew, the box of Mallomars was moving across the checkout belt in first place. That just reminded me that I was in fourth place, and in my house, being the one in fourth place is the same as being invisible.

But even Mushy's Mallomars could not stop my brain from thinking of new inventions, and I had two more ideas before I went to bed that night. The first was a Page Turner for my book. I don't know which is stickier, my hands or my book, but I always seem to turn more than one page at a time. And the second was a dog tunnel that would lead from my bedroom window to the yard. Chunky could run straight down there whenever he needed to go out. And he could come back in, independently, when he was ready. My life would be so much easier because I wouldn't have to go downstairs, open the door, wait, and let him back inside.

I went over my inventions in my head.

MIND-READING MACHINE

CHINA DOGS WITH OPPOSABLE THUMBS

HIDDEN-SCALE PLATE

PLUG-IN FUZZIES

COLLAR-&-CRIB SYSTEM

AUTOMATIC DRESSER

CONVERTIBLE LAP SEAT

PAGE TURNER FOR BOOKS

WINDOW DOG TUNNEL

CHAPTER SEVEN

MUCKERS

Mrs. Howdy Doody was wearing a tracksuit when I got to school the next day, and she didn't have on her slippers. She had on sneakers, big, red sneakers, and she was jogging in place. I had never seen somebody so old move so lightly.

"Attention, muckers!" Mrs. Howdy Doody called out, once we all sat down. "That's what Thomas Edison called his workers!" I decided right then that I liked Thomas Edison, because "mucker" was a very funny word.

"Can anybody guess why I'm wearing my tracksuit?"

Donnie raised his hand and said, "Kickball?"

"That's a worthy answer," said Mrs. Howdy Doody, "and I do love kickball. But that's not why I'm wearing these clothes."

I rolled my eyes over to the right and noticed that Foster Brooks was nodding. He must be interested in muckers, or exercise, or both.

"'Genius is one percent inspiration,'" said Mrs. Howdy Doody, moving her hands up

47

like a conductor, "'and ninety-nine percent perspiration'! That is a quote from Mr. Edison. He meant that inventors have to keep working on their ideas all the time."

I sure didn't mind working on my ideas—it wouldn't be possible for me to stop working! In fact, I was just sitting there innocently looking at Mrs. Howdy Doody's feet when another idea popped into my head. Sneaker-slippers. I could call them Sneapers. They would be furry and plushy on top, with running-shoe bottoms. Mrs. Howdy Doody could be my first customer!

And as if she had purchased my Mind-Reading Machine, Mrs. Howdy Doody started jogging around the room, motioning for us to follow. "Rise up, dear muckers!" she said. "It's time to perspire. It's time to sweat!"

I don't know how it happened, but I ended up right behind Foster Brooks, which meant I could watch him without getting the scissors again. The only bad part was that I couldn't see his face while he was jogging, and I was kind of curious what he thought about Mrs. Howdy Doody, since he couldn't possibly be used to her yet.

His yellow T-shirt had a smiley face on the back exactly like the smiley face I'd seen on the front. And it said TEAM SMILEY FACE, just like the front too. We didn't have a team called that at Lambert Elementary, so I wondered if this was some kind of special team he was on at his old school, and that made me wonder where his old school was, and why he had moved, and whether or not he had any siblings. There was so much I didn't know about Foster Brooks. . . . If he had chosen his shirt himself, he might be friendly, but if his mother picked it for him, who knows? Just like with the scissors he made at me. If he'd meant cut it out, he might be funny, but if he'd meant he wanted to cut my head off, he might be angry. His pants were brown, and his sneakers were blue—which all seemed regular, but the shirt was strange. I couldn't tell what kind of socks he had on, and I was afraid that if I tried to look down there, he'd notice. After the second trip around the room, my forehead felt sweaty—I guess Mrs. Howdy Doody meant it when she said it was time to perspire.

"Thomas Edison worked very hard," said Mrs. Howdy Doody, "but he was famous for saying he was having fun the whole time. And now I hope you are inspired to perspire too! Your final list of inventions is due on Monday. Have a wonderful time!"

I was willing to make a bet with myself that I'd win this contest. It was going to be a piece o' cake. And I didn't even think I was going to sweat . . . at least not as much as I did during Mrs. Howdy Doody's "pep rally"!

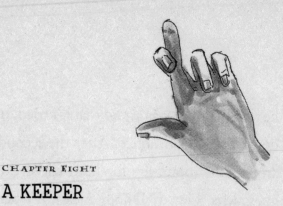

CHAPTER EIGHT

A KEEPER

"Big news," said Pam when I walked in the door from school. "You're going to meet McQuade tonight."

"The McQuade?" I said. I couldn't believe I was finally going to meet Pam's boyfriend!

"He wants to go to Fondue," she said.

"With Charlie and the Bea—"

"I know," said Pam. "But he asked. He wants to get to know the people I'm spending my weekends with."

I wouldn't exactly call the Beasties

"people," and I was guessing that even though Pam had probably warned McQuade about them, they would still scare him.

Sometimes you like somebody because they like you first, and that's what happened to me with McQuade. Chunky and I were in my room when Chunky started dig-crunching. It sounds a tiny bit like digging and a tiny bit like crunching, and it means that Chunky is excited, but he doesn't want to leave my room without me. (He has always had good manners.) I looked out the window and I saw a man, in a long gray coat with a red woolly scarf, getting out of his car. *Now* I knew why Chunky was dig-crunching. This must be McQuade. He was coming in the front door as I was going down the stairs, and he had green eyes that were as sparkly as diamonds. He swooshed right up to me, lifted me down the stairs, raised my hand in the air, and twirled me. And even though I'd never met him before, I knew right then and there that he was a gentleman.

When he finished twirling me one way, he twirled me the other way—it was almost like his hand could give me directions.

And after three twirls his hand made me stop, and he said, "You must be Dessert," with a voice that sounded like he should be in the back row of the choir.

"How did you do that?" I said.

"It's all in the hand," he said back. He must

have something in his hand that I couldn't see or feel, because nobody had ever twirled me like that. I'd have to remember to write down "Hand Twirler" in my notebook, because if I could invent something that twirled people

so smoothly, I would be a multimillionaire. It made me feel like a celebrity!

And then Charlie and Wolfie and Mushy and Pam came up from the basement, and he twirled each of them the same way. He kissed Pam on the cheek, and I saw her face turn a little red, the same way Foster's had the first day he came to our school.

"Are you going to get married?" I asked.

"Save your questions for later," McQuade replied, and I noticed that Pam's face had turned bright red. She looked like a fire engine!

A very short while later we were at Fondue. I had never been there on a Friday night before. Mummy was just inside the door, and she was glowing. At first I thought she might be happy to see me, but then I took a look around, and I knew why she was happy—because Fondue was packed full of customers. That's why Daddy calls it a "destination restaurant." There must have been a hundred and fifty covers!

Guston, our headwaiter, was in a hurry. And when he kissed each of us on both cheeks, it was like somebody had pressed fast-forward on him—I'm not sure he even touched my face! Guston picked up high chairs for Wolfie and Mushy, and we were at our table, Number Twelve, in less than a minute. I got to sit by McQuade.

I did what I always do first—check the little sheet inside my menu that tells me today's special dessert fondue flavor. It was Marble Meltaway. That's a good one, and it tastes like a soft-twist ice-cream cone of chocolate and vanilla, except that it's very warm, and very gooey. No wonder the line at the tower was so long!

I could see the back of Mummy from our table, and she kept greeting more and more people. And though I couldn't see her face, I could tell from the way her head was nodding that she was saying, "Good evening."

"Tell me what to order," McQuade said to me, and I told him what we have every time we go to our restaurant.

"It's called the flight," I said. "You start with cheese fondue, which is cooked right at your table, and you end up with a trip to the tower." I pointed to the Eiffel Fondue Tower. "See that line?" I said. McQuade nodded. "That's for the Marble Meltaway Fondue." I pointed to the little sheet and said, "The dessert." And before I could say any more, Gaby arrived at our table.

"Gaby!" I said. "This is McQuade." I felt proud to introduce him. "We'll have the usual." Next to Guston, who's like a relative, Gaby's my favorite server, because she's nice and she knows some really good jokes.

"Coming right up," said Gaby, and she didn't even write down our order. She just put her notepad in her apron pocket and moved on to her next table.

"Can I see your hand?" I said to McQuade.

McQuade gave me his hand. It was large, and it had some black hair on the outside. I took his index finger and I bent it a little. "Does that hurt?" I said. He shook his head. "Good," I said. Then I put his middle finger over his index finger, and I asked, "How does that feel?"

"Okay," he said.

"Keep them crossed like that," I said. "For good luck!" I turned my head a little bit toward Pam, but not enough so she would notice.

Before he could say anything back, Gaby came over with our bread, but she didn't look like herself. Her eyebrows were close together.

"I don't know what to do," she said.

"What's wrong?" asked Pam.

"It's the people in front," said Gaby. "He went to bring his car up for his parents, but he can't start it. His battery's dead."

"Are there jumper cables in the van?" McQuade asked, standing up. "I can get his car going." A second later Pam was putting the keys in McQuade's hand. He held them up and turned to Gaby. "I'd like to help," he said.

"Are you sure?" she asked, and I could see from her eyebrows that she was relieved.

"Let's go," he said. And the next thing I saw was McQuade leaving the restaurant with the man who needed help. Gaby came back to our table and leaned down to Pam. "He's a keeper," she said. And Pam turned into a fire engine again.

"I'll be back with your cheddar," said Gaby.

"What's a 'keeper'?" I asked Pam.

And Pam said, "Shhhhhhhhh," and

reached over and put her hand on my mouth. "Behave," she said.

By the time Gaby came back with our food, McQuade was sitting down again.

"Your customers are on their way home," he said.

Pam's eyes looked proud, and Gaby said, "Thank you." She set up our fondue pot, and lit the Sterno (it's like a squishy blue candle in a can that heats up the fondue). She threw some garlic into the pot and started stirring. Then she added some mustard.

"I'll do the cheese," I said, and Gaby handed me the shredded cheese. I dumped it in.

"Now a little wine," she said, as she

poured in the wine. She kept stirring until the fondue was thick and bubbly. "You may be the critic," Gaby said to McQuade, and she handed him the bowl of bread. I knew Gaby was giving McQuade an honor, but he looked confused.

"Like this," I said, and took his skewer and put a big piece of bread on it. Then I rolled it around in the pot until it looked like a Super Ball.

"Try it," I said.

McQuade put the Super Ball in his mouth, and his eyes gleamed. I wondered if he'd ever had fondue before. When he finished, he said, "It's delicious."

Gaby looked at Pam and made a thumbs-up. Pam looked over at me, and I made one too. I still wasn't sure what a "keeper" was, but I figured it meant that if your boyfriend knows how to make a dead car battery come alive, and he really likes fondue, too, you should keep him around. Pam's face was a fire engine *again*, and I was pretty sure that meant she thought he was a keeper too.

CHAPTER NINE

IN WHICH FOSTER SPEAKS

On Monday Mrs. Howdy Doody was wearing a different colored tracksuit, and our desks were pushed together in groups of two. I sat down, and I was face-to-face with Evan. This was kind of a relief, even though I wasn't sure what we'd be doing. I'd rather have his brainpower on my team than on somebody else's.

Sharon sat down a few seats away, and she was with Foster Brooks, which was also good, because she could tell me what he's really like—I'd be able to find out more about him without staring. I checked where Bonnie was, and it looked like she had Jeanne S., who's an artist. She draws on the top of her desk with her finger all the time—other than that, she's pretty normal.

Mrs. Howdy Doody clapped for attention, and when the room was quiet, she said, "From the time he was a little boy, Thomas Edison asked a lot of questions, dear muckers. Now it's our turn!" She drew a big question mark on the board. "Why, just this morning," she said, "as I was thinking about my Reversible Car, I asked myself what I would do if I wanted to drive from the back instead of the front. I'd have to open the front door, get out, close the front door, walk to the back of the car, open the back door, sit down behind the steering wheel, close the back door, and put on my seat belt—all before driving forward from the back." I went over what she was saying in my head, and it seemed really complicated, but each step was necessary.

Mrs. Howdy Doody continued, "Then I asked myself what would happen if somebody was driving behind me, just when I needed to switch from front to back." And that's when Foster Brooks raised his hand. When he was called on, he stood up, put his hands on his hips, and sang, in a clear voice,

"BEEP, BEEPY-BEEP-BEEP, BEEP BEEP!"

Everybody, including Mrs. Howdy Doody, began to laugh. Nobody expected that from Foster. His hand wave and scissor cuts were kind of funny, but I didn't know he was a comedian—I didn't even know he could talk!

"You're exactly right, Foster!" Mrs. Howdy Doody said. "And that's why I decided that my Reversible Car might not improve my life after all! It might be better to practice my parking than to drive a Reversible Car.

"And now it's your turn, dear muckers! Each of you has a Question Partner, and each of you may submit only *one* of your inventions into the contest. Ask each other questions, and help each other decide which inventions will improve our lives the most!"

How would I ever choose just one invention from my list? If only Mrs. Howdy Doody
would make an exception and let me submit
all of mine.

CHAPTER TEN

MY QUESTION PARTNER

"Ladies first," Evan said, and that made me laugh. There are some people who mean to be funny, and others who just *are* funny, and Evan just *is* funny. Guston is like that too.

The first invention on my list was the Mind-Reading Machine, and I skipped right over it, because now that I thought about it, I only liked the idea of *me* being able to read other people's minds—I didn't want them to be able to read mine. That brought me to China Dogs with Opposable Thumbs.

But I didn't really want Evan to know that I play with china dogs. I wanted to keep that to myself. "You can go," I said, because I'd crossed my first two inventions off my list without saying a thing.

"Mine is the Flying Car I told you about on the bus," said Evan.

"I remember that," I said, "but I don't really get how it works."

"Have you ever used a zip line before?" he asked. I nodded, because I rode a zip line at camp, and I zoomed across the wire so fast I decided I would never do it again.

"Well, it works kind of like that," he said. "But the zip line is magnetic. The car is magnetic, too. So the zip line repels the car, and that keeps it in the air." I didn't really get it until Evan showed me a picture that looked like telephone poles and wires with cars hovering above.

"That looks like a cool invention," I said, "and if your car is in the air, you won't get into a traffic jam." Since none of us has a license yet, I didn't really think it would make our lives that much easier. But he was so absorbed

in his science that I didn't say anything. It was just comforting to know he wasn't going to win.

"Hidden-Scale Plate," I said next. Evan asked me if it would be dishwasher safe. I wasn't sure about that, so I crossed it off my list.

Plug-In Fuzzies was my next one, so I told Evan about them.

"Do you sleep on your stomach, or on your side?" he asked. I started to tell him that I move around all night, but before I finished, I realized why he had asked me that. Because nobody wants to sleep on an extension-cord plug. Crud.

"Let's move on," I said. "Your turn."

"I'm focusing on the Flying Car," said Evan. "Look." He opened his notebook, and he had way more pictures than the telephone-wire sketch he showed me. He had actually filled his notebook with diagrams. . . . I saw some fractions in there too, and also quite a few graphs. I felt a little sorry for him, putting all his hope on something that wasn't going to make our lives that much better.

"Okay," I said, "that's a lot of work. Let me show you my Collar-&-Crib System." After I explained how it worked just like a dog fence, Evan said that even though electric crib bars might make my life easier, they were inhumane, because the Beasties might accidentally roll into them during the night

77

and that could wake them up when they were trying to sleep, and that I might possibly end up in jail for using them. So I crossed it off my list. Every single one of my first five inventions had been crossed out—I guess the quality wasn't quite as high as I hoped, but I still had plenty left. . . .

The Automatic Dresser was next, and Evan said that drawers locking in connection with the weather might be hard to engineer. And I'm not sure if it was the fact that I didn't want to cross another invention off my list, or that I wanted a snack, but that's

78

when I thought of my grandest invention of all. It was based on the Automatic Dresser, but it would look like a vending machine.

"I've got it!" I said to Evan. "I'm calling it the Vending Dresser."

Evan looked confused, so I opened my notebook and made a quick sketch. "It looks like a soda machine," I said. "But it's full of clothes. Each outfit will be in a different little window, and every morning you can press a button to get your clothes without even using money."

"What about the weather?" said Evan.

"Piece o' cake!" I said. "The outfits will be changed for each season—spring, summer, fall, and winter."

"What if you don't care what clothes you wear?" Evan asked.

"Even better," I said. "You can just close your eyes and press a button."

"Will socks be included?" Evan asked.

"With every outfit!" I said.

"My mother will love that," said Evan. "It sounds all right to me." Evan was the best Question Partner in the world. Not only did he ask me plenty of questions like Thomas Edison would have, but if it weren't for him, my first five inventions would still be on my list, and my mind would never have created the Vending Dresser. My visionary brain cells were working overtime. A Vending Dresser would definitely make people's lives easier, and I would not end up in jail.

I didn't really even want to go through the rest of my list, because I already had the winner, but it was part of the assignment. Evan didn't really understand about the Convertible Lap Seat because he's an only child, and he told me he thought a Page Turner for Books had already been invented. He was also afraid that Chunky might have a tough time getting back up the Window Dog Tunnel. And when I told him about the Hand Twirler, he said I'd need a neurologist to figure that one out. That sounded expensive. As for Sneapers, Evan said that even though they were fun and different, they weren't practical. He was right.

I was grateful that my Question Partner had troubleshooted away all my ideas because I had come up with something new. There was no way anybody would have a better invention than mine. Before the end of the day, Mrs. Howdy Doody said, "A final drawing of your invention is due on Wednesday. Good luck to you all, dear muckers!"

On the bus home, Sharon told us that she didn't really get any helpful questions, because all Foster did was make jokes. "He made fun of my Doll-Clothes Washer," she said. Then she told us that when she tried to tell him about it, all he did was start moving his head in a circle, and he kept saying he was getting dizzy.

"That doesn't sound very nice," I said to Sharon. "What did he invent?" And Sharon told me that Foster's invention was Zoo Noses. They were a collection of zoo-animal noses made out of sponges. You could hook them onto your own nose without using tape, glue, or string.

"That's not going to make people's lives easier," I said. "I think your idea's better, and I bet the people who make Barbie dolls would buy it." Then I patted Sharon on the shoulder. I started thinking they might buy a miniature Vending Dresser, too!

Bonnie said things had gone okay with Jeanne, although all she did was draw pictures of what Bonnie said. When Bonnie

83

told Jeanne about her Twenty-Three-Dollar Bill invention, Jeanne drew it with Bonnie's face instead of the president's. That sounded really funny, even though that's not what a Question Partner was supposed to do. Maybe I should show Jeanne my Vending Dresser— she might put it on a *hundred*-twenty-three-dollar bill, and now that I thought about it, I bet my invention could sell for at least that much!

CHAPTER ELEVEN

IN WHICH DADDY FORGETS HER

I couldn't get the Vending Dresser out of my head. Just like Thomas Edison, I was about to face the unknown and make it known. It was impossible to calculate how many people's lives would be improved. I was going to win the Thomas Edison Contest! There was no doubt in my mind that Daddy's visionary genes had been passed down directly to me, and I wanted to get started drawing up my invention right away. Maybe Daddy would want to help me. He'd be home tonight, and he had promised to make me burritos. But maybe I'd ask him to help me with the Vending Dresser instead. Who knows what might happen when two visionaries got together?

"I thought you had Enrichment today," Mummy said when I walked in the door.

"Next week," I said. "Where's Dad?"

"Catering," said Mummy. "He went to drop off the food."

"But I wanted to show him my invention," I said, "and he promised me burritos."

"You can show him later," Mummy said. "We'll have burritos tomorrow."

Mummy didn't even ask to see my invention, and I didn't want burritos *tomorrow*— Daddy had promised them to me today. He said he would make them especially for me.

The truth is that when your mother doesn't know your schedule, and your father doesn't remember he promised you something, and then your mother doesn't ask about your invention, you feel like keeping to

yourself. And that's how I felt right now. So I took a cheese stick out of the fridge, and I said, "I'm going upstairs." Mummy would be sorry she didn't find out about my Vending Dresser, especially when she discovered how much it could improve her life. And I didn't want Daddy's help anymore. He'd find out all about the Vending Dresser when I won the contest. They'd both be sorry then.

CHAPTER TWELVE

THE VENDING DRESSER

I wanted my Vending Dresser to look as much like a vending machine as possible. Everybody I know likes to press a button and get something (including me!). It needed noises like a pinball machine, for when the outfit drops down. One outfit would be in each window, hanging on a hook in a ziplock bag. When a button for an outfit was pressed, the hook would tilt down and drop the ziplock bag. At exactly the same time, bells and noises would go off like fireworks. You would feel as if you were winning a game at a carnival! Then you could reach in the bottom and get your outfit. And I had another special bonus idea! After you took your outfit, the machine would say, "Have a good-lookin' day!" What was I going to think of next?

It was just perfect. You wake up, take off your pajamas, walk over to your dresser, press a button, hear some winning sounds, watch your outfit drop off its hook, reach in the bottom, hear a voice tell you to have a good-lookin' day ☺, open your ziplock bag, get dressed, and go downstairs for breakfast. A computer person (maybe even Evan!) could design a way to allow only one outfit to drop every day. And if I folded the clothes really tightly, the compartments inside the Vending Dresser wouldn't have to be very big. I could fit four windows across and five down. Five times four is twenty, which is exactly how many school days are in a month! My magnificent machine would hold a full month's supply of school clothes. And it *would* be just like a Coke machine with the buttons and everything.

I'd have a girls' model, a boys' model, and a self-serve model. In the girls' model, each compartment could have socks or tights, underwear, and either a dress (if there were tights) or pants and a shirt. The pants and shirts would be for gym days, or also if you didn't like dresses (you could have the choice of all pants if you were a pants-only person). The boys' model could also have socks and underwear, plus pants and shirts. There could be turtlenecks for cold winter months, and short sleeves for warmer weather. The self-serve model could be offered at a lower price—you buy the Vending Dresser but fill it with your own clothes. That could be good for people who prefer to put together their own outfits. As I was thinking about how fantastic it would be to hear sounds as the clothes dropped, I realized I should also make the buttons light up, and I'd have to figure out a way to use different colors

for the lights (I bet Evan could help again!).
This would attract customers, and it also made
sense for the Thomas Edison Contest,
with the long-burning lightbulb Mrs.
Howdy Doody talked about and
everything. And Charlie couldn't
borrow my clothes anymore. Not
even my socks! The Vending Dresser
would be ideal for households with
lots of children who don't like to share. Another
selling point!

I could just imagine what my parents
would say when I won. They might want to
have a party for me. It was time for them to
recognize my abilities. If you
can't get a pat on the back from

your own parents, who can you turn to? I made a detailed drawing, and I used a ruler to make sure my twenty squares were straight. I numbered them one to twenty and drew a button to press for each one. Next I drew ten bells sitting on top with sound lines to show there was noise. In the middle of the bells, as a centerpiece, I drew a big smiley face, with a talk bubble that said, "Have a good-lookin' day!"

And then I began to color. Luckily, I have 128 crayons in my box, and I used as many of them as I could, because the way I see it, I wouldn't have to make the dresser available in different colors if I used enough of them. It might almost look like a painted sculpture.

And now that I was thinking about it, I figured that once my dressers were selling well, I could make them for grown-ups, too. It seems like Mummy is always digging around in her closet or running off to the dry cleaner, and this could really help her.

When I finished, I wrote on the top of my sheet, the Vending Dresser. Then I signed my name.

by Dessert

I showed my final drawing to Chunky, and his eyes lit up, just like the buttons on my dresser would when it was manufactured! And then I tucked it carefully into my backpack. If my parents weren't interested in me, then they didn't deserve to see my amazing invention. They'd have enough to do very soon, planning my victory party!

CHAPTER THIRTEEN

NO COMPETITION

When I got dressed the next morning, I wished I already had my Vending Dresser, because all my pants were dirty, which meant I was going to have to wear a dress on a gym day. My pants were dirty because they were sitting in a little nest in my closet. When Mummy checks my room to see if it's picked up, she never looks in my closet, as long as the door to it is closed. That's because she likes things tidy, but she doesn't do research. It occurred to me that there were probably a lot of other kids in the same situation I was in. That made me all the more hopeful that I was going to win. Every kid with a nest of dirty clothes in their closet would be better off with my Vending Dresser.

So I put on my red sweaterdress, and I started digging for some clean tights. There weren't any. I was going to have to wear socks with bare legs and it wasn't summertime—I'd have to sneak past Mummy. She would not like this. I woke up Charlie and went down to the kitchen to eat my breakfast. I kept close to the counter so that Mummy couldn't see my legs. But she didn't even look up at me—she was already on the phone and she just pointed to the table, where a small bowl of oatmeal was waiting for me. Why had I even thought she would look at me?

After my breakfast I got up and marched right past her, called for Chunky, yelled good-bye to whoever might hear it, and before I knew it, I was face-to-face with Mrs. Howdy Doody, and she handed me a clothespin. (She was

wearing the same tracksuit that she wore last week, and that made me think that she could use a Vending Dresser too.) My desk was still across from Evan, so I sat down. Without speaking, Evan pointed toward the window, and that's when I noticed the wire running around our whole room, almost like a fence for cows. First I thought it might be for his Flying Car, but then I looked at my clothespin, and I knew, without being told, that it wouldn't be long before I'd be introducing my Vending Dresser to the world.

"Attention, dear muckers!" Mrs. Howdy Doody said. "Here is my Reversible Car." She walked up to the wire and hung up a drawing. She'd added a little cartoon bubble that said, "Beep-Beepy-Beep-Beep!" That reminded me of Foster—who was wearing another smiley shirt today. The self-serve model would be perfect for him—he'd just fill it with smiley T-shirts and pants! Then Mrs. Howdy Doody told us that we would each have a chance to present our inventions. We would have a couple days to look over all the candidates, to think about which ones would improve our lives the most. On Friday, we'd cast our votes for the winner of the Thomas Edison Contest.

"Who would like to share first?" she said. Amy D. raised her hand.

"Proceed to the wire," said Mrs. Howdy Doody, "and tell us the name of your invention!"

Amy hung up a picture that looked kind of like a Halloween mask, but I couldn't tell exactly what it was. "I come from a horse family," she said, "and my invention is a modified horse blinder." She was looking right at me. "During a race, we use the blinders to keep our horses focused on what's in front of them, and that made me think they might be useful for humans, too." She pointed to the drawing. "The Human Blinders," she said, "will help prevent staring. This will improve our lives." Had she seen me staring at Foster Brooks? There was no way. And even if she had, she should have thought out her invention more. Because I'm sure I wasn't the only one who might like to see Amy D. wear the blinders herself.

103

Maybe I would make a special Vending Dresser just for her, with a set of disposable Human Blinders in each window like the 3-D glasses you get at the movies.

Geezy Lou was next, and her invention was Edible Lipstick. That sounded really good to me, and if it tasted like candy but didn't count as candy or dessert, it would make my life easier because I could eat more treats. But I didn't think she'd win because boys wouldn't vote for it. Evan announced his Flying Car, and everybody gasped. Sometimes people do that when other people are really smart. Still, it wasn't something we could drive ourselves, and I just didn't think he'd get the votes.

Billy invented a Two-Headed Water Gun

with a rearview mirror on it. You could shoot from either end. So if somebody came up behind you, you could squirt them without even turning around. It was so awesome, and people were clapping for him, but it seemed like it was more for fun, so I didn't think he'd win. Donnie had the same Two-Headed Water Gun with a rearview mirror, but his was filled with lemonade, and he wanted it to be a toy giveaway at McDonald's. He got a round of applause just like his brother.

Sharon showed her Doll-Clothes Washer next, and even though I loved it, I wasn't sure how many people would vote for her, because a lot of people don't play with dolls. The same with Pat D. and his Guinea-Pig

Racetrack—good idea, but hardly anybody has guinea pigs. And when Emily V. showed us her Healthy Gum, which was made by chewing a Red Delicious apple until it felt like gum, I knew she wouldn't win. I'd rather have no gum at all than a chawed apple peel.

And then it was my turn. It was my big chance. I walked right up to the wire and hung up my magnificent drawing. I paused between each word as I said,

"This

is

the

Vending

Dresser."

And then I explained exactly how it worked. "The Vending Dresser," I said, "contains twenty complete outfits, starting at the socks and ending with the shirt. It saves both time and money," I continued. Then I outlined the three different models and called attention to all the extras. When I finished, I said, "Vote for the Vending Dresser, because it's as fun as a soda machine, as noisy as a pinball machine, and it tells you to have a good-lookin' day every time you use it!" When I finished talking, I kind of wished I had that Mind-Reading Machine, because although it was quiet, I was sure everybody's mind was full of compliments for me, either that or my classmates were clapping in their brains. I started to think about whether my party should be at Fondue or at my house, and what we should have to eat—

"Dessert!" said Mrs. Howdy Doody. "Thank you for sharing!"

My eyes blinked wide when she spoke. How long had I been standing there? I guess it didn't even matter because my classmates were probably grateful to get more time to think about how much better their lives would be with their own Vending Dresser. So I just said, "You're welcome," and went to my desk.

Foster Brooks was next. I had heard about the Zoo Noses from Sharon, but what I saw caught me off guard. Foster was wearing a brown-bear nose.

He didn't say a word about it, though. He just walked up to the wire and held up his picture with one hand. At the top it said, ZOO NOSES, in big black letters, with drawings of different animal noses underneath. Then, like a silent clown, Foster underlined each word with his index finger and pointed to his "nose," as if he had something important to tell us. Everybody was laughing. I was wondering if he wanted to be an actor, because he was so good at performing. Now I know what Mummy means when she says Actions speak louder than Words. They're funnier, too.

I was actually a tiny bit worried Foster might get some votes. And he wasn't even finished. He flipped his picture over, and it said, NO TAPE. NO GLUE. NO STRING. People were clapping and laughing so hard—and even though Foster was funny, I had to believe they were trying to make him feel good because he was the new kid. But I also had to admit that I could have watched him forever—it was like he had his own special language, and an urgent message to tell us. He took off his bear nose and showed us the slit in the back. So that's what kept the nose on his face! It was such a simple idea. His Zoo Nose would fit any size person!

Then he did something I could never have guessed he would do. He walked to the front of the room, and he wrote "G-R-R-R-R" on the board. And then he used his Zoo Nose to wipe all of the letters off. Sharon was right when she said they were made of sponges. Sponge Zoo Noses were a great invention. Foster took a bow, and everybody laughed again. But in the end I decided there was no way he'd win, because he had ended his demonstration with cleaning up, and nobody likes to clean up. I didn't see how a Zoo Nose would make life better than a Vending Dresser, but still . . .

Tammy S. presented Precut Hot Dogs, which she planned to get approved by the government because they prevented choking, and I had to admit this was pretty smart, even though her mother must have thought of it. Still, I didn't think kids would buy it, just grown-ups. That reminded me, once again, how my invention was for all ages. And then came Jeanne S., and even though I didn't think it was really possible to make a Rainbow Peacock, it was the most beautiful painting I'd ever seen. She wasn't going to win the contest with that, but it was clear that she would be a famous artist someday. Charlotte R.'s paper said Healthy Computer, but there was no picture. That made me think that she hadn't actually done her homework. Because it seemed like she copied Emily's idea for Healthy Gum, but changed the last word. The good news was that Charlotte wasn't a threat. And Sam C. had stickers that looked like Band-Aids, which I didn't really understand because Band-Aids are already stickers—at least that's what Wolfie thinks.

Marshall W. had Remote-Control Condiments, which I thought was useful. Instead of saying, "Please pass the salt," at supper, you just pressed a button and the salt came walking over like a robot. I thought my parents might be interested in that—maybe they could have one saltshaker for the entire restaurant! Remote-Control Condiments would definitely improve people's lives, but it wasn't a real necessity like the Vending Dresser. So I wasn't worried.

Lois Z. showed us Heated Shorts, and she said they were good because even when it's not summer you could wear shorts. I didn't think this would work, because the rest of your legs would get cold, just like mine were right now. No competition there. And Jack S. had created a One-Man Golf Cart. He said it used less gas than a normal golf cart. At first it seemed like this would be good for the Earth, but I don't know how many people go golfing alone. And if they didn't go alone, then they might need a few

One-Man Golf Carts, and so it might not be so good for the Earth after all. Jack was not going to win, that's for sure.

Grace E. had a necklace with a crumb tray built in to it, so you could eat wherever you wanted to without getting caught. I thought this might be good for my dad because he leaves food all over his car, but I wasn't sure it would improve people's lives. It might increase the cost of groceries because everybody would just eat more. No worries there. Bonnie had chosen her Stretchy Arm invention over her Marshmallow Milk. She said it was excellent for taking food at the dinner table and also for the monkey bars. She added that it could be helpful for those who couldn't get around that well, too—you could keep your house and lawn neat without moving much. Both of these examples seemed like they would improve people's lives, but she made the same mistake Foster did by mentioning cleaning. That's one thing nobody likes to do!

Melissa, Michael, and Josh were the last to share, and Melissa had made Ben & Jerry's Toothpaste, which came in all the same flavors as Ben & Jerry's. I know that brand of ice cream, but I'd rather have real ice cream than ice-cream-flavored toothpaste. Other people would probably feel the same way. Michael had Meal-in-a-Pill. You could take the pill instead of eating a meal, so you wouldn't waste time, but that would put my parents out of business pretty quickly. Not an improvement. And Josh had a Universal On-Off Switch, so you could turn all the lights on or off in your house at the same time. I liked this idea but wasn't sure how good it was—you could waste electricity with lights on in rooms nobody is in.

I had to be honest with myself—the only person I was slightly concerned about was Foster Brooks, and it wasn't because of his invention—it was because everybody loved him. But I believed that the best invention would win over popularity, and there was not one invention up there as good as the Vending Dresser. I couldn't wait until Friday.

CHAPTER FOURTEEN

CANDLESTICKS

Then came gym class. And just as the morning had proved to me that there was no invention that would improve my life as much as the Vending Dresser, the afternoon proved to me just how badly I needed one. First of all, like clockwork, Mrs. Templar, my gym teacher, told me not to wear a dress on a gym day. Usually I would not like to be spoken to like that in front of all my classmates, especially Amy D., but I didn't mind today. Because Mrs. Templar was actually helping me win votes for the Vending Dresser. She was reminding everybody in my entire class what can happen when you don't have one.

Amy D. raised her hand, looked at me, and said, "Can you still pass third grade if you fail gym?"

I told Mrs. Templar I would have the proper clothes next time, and then I said to Amy, loud enough for everybody to hear, **"There's no need to fail if you have a Vending Dresser."** Nobody said anything back, most likely because they were already planning to vote for me.

Then Mrs. Templar announced that we were going to warm up with candlesticks. Let me explain. You lie on your back and put your legs in the air. Then you push your rear end up as high as it will go with your hands. I guess somebody must have decided this looks like a candlestick, though I'm not sure why they don't just call it a plain candle. Anyway, I didn't want to make one, because I didn't want anybody to see my rear end, and I didn't know how to hold it up and keep it covered by my dress at the same time.

I lay down on my back, and said, "If only I had a Vending Dresser, I'd have pants on today. . . ." But Mrs. Templar didn't say anything. So I raised my hand this time, and when she called on me, I said, "I can't do candlesticks today, Mrs. Templar. I wish I had a Vending Dresser!"

I made sure to say it loud enough for everybody to hear again, and that's when Mrs. Templar told me to go sit by the wall until we finished warm-ups. I almost didn't even mind, because I'd been able to call attention to my invention twice. They'd all remember the Vending Dresser long after they'd forgotten about Sponge Zoo Noses!

CHAPTER FIFTEEN

REASON TO BELIEVE

What happened that afternoon made me even *more* confident I'd win, because after school, as I was trying to do my homework, I heard a very loud crash. It sounded like thunder and a window shattering at the same time. It was coming from Wolfie's room. Mummy had said he was taking a nap, but that wasn't the truth, because about ten seconds later, he showed up in my doorway, and his wet blue eyes looked scared. He held his arms toward me, but he didn't say a thing, and I could see that he was trembling a tiny bit. Wolfie hardly ever trembles, and that made me want to protect him. I picked him up and wiped his eyes, and I said, "I'll fix it." Sometimes I really love that kid.

"Stay here," I said, putting him down. "I want you to be safe."

Then I walked into his room. He had pulled all three drawers out of his dresser, and the whole thing had crashed to the floor. That must have been the "thunder." I don't know how he escaped from his crib and got out of his room without hurting himself. This disaster made me think Evan was wrong about my Collar-&-Crib System after all. Wolfie's giant dinosaur snow globe was now a pile of wet

glass and colored grains of sand. The dinosaur didn't have a head anymore, either.

Mummy came in, and I said, "Wolfie needs a Vending Dresser."

"Right," she replied, setting the dresser back up on its legs and pushing one of the drawers back in.

"Please get the vacuum," Mummy said back, as she pushed the gooey snow-globe glass into a pile.

She hadn't heard a single word that had come out of my mouth, so I said, "Sure," because I wasn't going to let another day of being ignored ruin the confident feeling I had. By the end of the week, she'd find out just how "right" I really was. When I came home and announced that I'd won the Thomas Edison Contest with my Vending Dresser, she'd regret that she hadn't paid more attention to me.

I went over all the reasons I should win as I went to get the vacuum. First, there was all the time that would be saved in choosing your clothing in the morning, and like Mummy always says, "Time is money." I'm sure Thomas Edison felt that way too. Also, for people who were supposed to help their siblings get dressed, the Vending Dresser would pretty much guarantee a problem-free morning. Second, the Vending Dresser held a full month's worth of school clothes. No more water wasted from washing too many clothes. So it was good for the Earth in its own way. You'd only have to do your laundry once a month. Third, there would be no more candlesticks kind of problems. Fourth, and just as important as everything else, pressing buttons and hearing noises was a big attraction. And the "Have a good-lookin' day!" message was just icing on the cake! No way would someone choose a Zoo Nose over my dresser. In fact, those extras on my Vending Dresser might even make it a destination in your own home, like the Eiffel Fondue Tower at our restaurant. As I hauled the vacuum up the stairs, I was more convinced than ever before that good news was heading my way.

CHAPTER SIXTEEN

LET THERE BE LIGHTBULBS

On Friday, when I arrived at school, it seemed like Election Day to me. Mrs. Howdy Doody, who was wearing her tracksuit again, handed me a ballot. It was about the size of a recipe card, and it said:

After a careful review
of the candidates,
I hereby cast my vote for

_____

Voting day was finally here! And even though I knew in my heart I was going to win, I still felt jumpy. I was so close to the victory party, and the more I thought about it, the more I wanted my whole class (except Amy D.) to be invited to our restaurant. We could invent a new fondue just for the party—maybe it could be called Lightbulb Lemon! Most people like lemon squares, and this kind of fondue would taste like shortbread and lemon meringue pie all mixed together! If only Thomas Edison were here to taste it.

A little while later Mrs. Howdy Doody told us that we could take a few minutes to review the candidates one final time, and then we could cast our vote. "Remember," she said, "to consider which invention will improve our lives the most. That is the Edison way!" I kind of felt like she was doing a personal advertising campaign for me. And I didn't have to pay for it! I put my ballot in my pocket and got in line to take one last look. I didn't want it to be too obvious that I was planning to vote for myself.

The final review was more like a parade, but it came to a stop around Foster's Zoo Noses. That's because he was standing there with the bear nose on again, and people were laughing (again). He was growling, too, and reaching around with his "claws." But when he bent over to walk like a real bear, his Zoo

Nose flew off. Everybody bent down to help him find it, and I squatted down too. There it was, right next to my shoe. People were still searching—that meant they hadn't seen it, so I slid my foot over and squished it. Then I just kept my foot in place as everybody kept looking. When nobody could find Foster's nose, the group began to break up and move on, so I simply bent down and "tied" my shoe. While I was doing that, I gently pressed the Zoo Nose into a tiny ball and slid it right into my pocket. Now Foster wouldn't be able to keep promoting his invention when we were supposed to be doing our final review.

Gradually the line got moving again and Foster got in it—I guess he didn't

131

feel like growling without a Zoo Nose on. He would definitely need to refine his invention so it stayed on his nose. . . . The line began to move quickly now, almost as if each person had already decided. I could relate to that. You didn't have to be a brain surgeon to know which invention would improve your life the most, especially now that Foster couldn't distract us.

Once we were all sitting down again, Mrs. Howdy Doody told us to fill out our ballots. This was a piece o' cake. I wrote:

After a careful review
of the candidates,
I hereby cast my vote for
The Vending Dresser

Everybody else was fast, too, and that could really mean only one thing—Lightbulb Lemon Fondue for all!

Mrs. Howdy Doody reached under her desk and came back up with a giant yellow box. It had a big slit in the top, and if I didn't know it was for our ballots, I would have thought it was the most gigantic, weirdest piggy bank I'd ever seen.

"It's time to cast your vote," she said to all of us. "Come forth, dear muckers, and place your ballots in this box!" I wanted to run to the front of the room to put my ballot in first, but I waited my turn like everybody else—it had been a long journey to get to today, and I was wise enough to know that a few more minutes would not hurt my chances of winning.

Sure enough, my turn came quickly, and I put my ballot in the box. When we all finished and were sitting back down, Mrs. Howdy Doody started counting the votes—I noticed right away that she was making two piles, and I didn't like the look of that. I must not have gotten every vote. Then she made a few more piles, and I didn't like the look of that *at all*.

She looked up at us and said, "This is a tight race!" And I think she gave me a special smile. I nodded my head just a little to let her know I got the message. When she finished counting, she closed our blinds, and our room got a little bit darker. I wondered if she was going to show a movie. Then she turned off the lights, and our room got much darker. I was getting butterflies. . . . Then Mrs. Howdy Doody turned on a flashlight . . . shined it on Donnie . . . and said,

"LET THERE BE
LIGHTBULBS!"

"With six votes," she said, "the winner of the Thomas Edison Contest is Donnie Blackett for his Two-Headed Lemonade Water Gun! Let's hear it for Donnie!"

I felt like I belonged in a wax museum. Even though I really liked Donnie, I couldn't move my hands to clap. It was hard to breathe, too.

"The Two-Headed Lemonade Water Gun," said Mrs. Howdy Doody, "will add so much fun to your lives! And doesn't having fun improve your life?" The air just kept coming up from my belly and wouldn't go out of my mouth. I felt like I was choking.

I had not won the contest. I. Had. Not. Won. The. Contest. IHADNOT WONTHECONTEST. IHADNOT WONTHE CONTEST. IHADNOT

WONTHECONTEST.
IHADNOTWON
THECONTEST
IHADNOTWON
THECONTEST
IHADNOTWON
CRUDCRUDCRUD
CRUDCRUD
CRUDDY
CRUDCRUD

CRUD!

I had blown my chance to become important. I had thought a little about fun, but not a lot about fun. Bells and lights and getting dressed were not as much fun as squirting somebody behind you in the mouth with lemonade. I felt about the size of my pinkie finger, and my brain felt smaller than that. I wasn't a visionary at all. Donnie deserved to win the most votes. There was no denying that. It was the truth.

"Hold your applause, dear muckers, until I've announced the runners-up," said Mrs. Howdy Doody. "There's a tie for second place. Five votes each went to Billy Blackett with the regular Two-Headed Water Gun and Foster Brooks with his Zoo Noses!" I could hardly breathe, and I had a very small brain at this point, but I could still do math. Seventeen votes were already accounted for; that meant that hardly anybody could possibly have voted for the Vending Dresser. Foster Brooks had tied for second, even though his invention was sitting in my pocket. It didn't feel so good to have the Zoo Nose right now. In fact, however I looked at the situation, I felt bad. Crud. Crud. Crud. Not very many people liked my idea, and even though I thought Foster had cheated, I had kind of cheated too. And who could blame them for not voting for me?

Who wants to press a button on a fake vending machine to get an outfit when you could shoot somebody with lemonade by eyeing them up in a mini rearview mirror? Nobody would choose clothes over that; not even me.

"Third Place goes to Marshall W. for the Remote-Control Condiments. He received three votes!" I let some breath out of my mouth. I hadn't even won third. Marshall's invention was cool, though I never thought anyone would vote for him. But salt- and pepper shakers that could move by pressing a button were better than getting clothes, too. More crud. There wouldn't be any Lightbulb Lemon Fondue streaming down from the tower any time soon.

"And fourth place goes to Dessert Schneider with two votes for the Vending Dresser." Two lousy votes . . . Election Day was turning out to be one of the worst days of my life, but at least one person besides me had voted for my boring invention. "And fifth place," said Mrs. Howdy Doody, "goes to Amy D., with one vote for the Human Blinders!" The tiny bit better I felt disappeared when I heard Amy D.'s name. She had probably voted for herself too.

I thought I was going to win by a landslide, but

instead I had been just one vote ahead of Amy D., and I had stolen Foster's Zoo Nose to try to get ahead. My lungs felt like they were stuffed with marbles. Maybe Mrs. Howdy Doody would leave the lights off. My parents were right to ignore me—I wasn't worth much attention.

I couldn't even be mad at Donnie and Billy. They're my friends, and their water-gun idea was tremendous, but I didn't think I'd be able to congratulate them today. I didn't think I'd be able to talk at all.

"We can only have one winner," Mrs. Howdy Doody said. "That's the nature of a contest." She put her hands in the steering-wheel position again, and "turned" it from side to side. "Remember this," she continued. "If you only look to the left or right," she said, "you forget to go forward." And she "drove" forward right around the room. "As the great man and thinker Thomas Edison might very well say if he were here with us today, there are no failures. There are only many worthy inventions that did not win." She "drove" in a straight line right up to the wire, and she said, "Keep driving forward."

Then she called Donnie to the front, and Mrs. Howdy Doody gave him a trophy. It was on a wooden base, and it was a lightbulb, and you could turn it on and off. He looked so proud.

I did my best to make a smile, but my lips

wouldn't stretch out to the sides. All I could think about was my stupid invention and the squishy thing in my pocket. And I didn't need to worry about the left or the right, and I didn't need to think about going forward, either, because I wasn't going anywhere at all.

CHAPTER SEVENTEEN

MY SAD TALENTS

On the bus, Sharon said, "I voted for you." That meant that only Sharon and I had voted for the Vending Dresser, and she was just being nice.

Bonnie said, "If your dresser had soda and not clothes, I would have voted for you, too."

Evan didn't say a thing. How could I have thought everybody was going to choose clothes over a cool toy? Why hadn't it occurred to me that a toy could improve your life so much more than clothes? It seemed obvious now. That's how we keep the Beasties busy half the time. Charlie, too. And I myself like toys. I felt so dumb for getting caught up in my own idea, when the real winner was a good friend of mine.

By the time I got home, I couldn't even say hi to McQuade, who was there again with Pam. I went right to my room.

Why had I even thought anybody would care about what they wore? And why had I even thought that other parents would let their kids run out of clean pants to wear? Most parents probably washed their kids' dirty clothes on a regular basis, whether they were in a nest in the closet or not. But not mine. Here

148

I thought I'd be coming home with the light-bulb trophy Donnie was probably showing to his mom right now, and I had only two things to say for myself—that I got two votes—one from myself and one from somebody who felt sorry for me—and that I had something in my pocket I wish wasn't there.

I started to think about all the other things I stink at, and even though Chunky gave me a big lick, I didn't feel better. All my friends are so good at stuff, and I'm only good at thinking about myself. Sharon can make doll clothes from her mom's old dresses, and even without her Stretchy Arms, Bonnie can do the monkey bars faster than anybody in the whole third grade. I sometimes think she might be part chimp. Evan is just an expert at being an expert—I couldn't remember ever asking him a question he couldn't answer. Billy and Donnie can do a lot more than place first and second in the Thomas Edison Contest. They can do handsprings, and Donnie can drum with his feet better than anybody—he can do it softly, even with his shoes on. And Emily, with her unpopular Healthy Gum, has the best handwriting in the world.

No wonder nobody liked me. I really only had sad talents.

My Sad Talents
I can't fall asleep in the car.
I don't like babysitting.

I stole today.
I can't make my tongue touch
   my nose.
I can't whistle.
I can't do straight cartwheels.
I'm afraid of bees.
I can't keep my room neat.
And I only think about myself,
   which is how this whole
   catastrophe started.

   I lay down on my rug to try to forget about
today, and that's when McQuade found me.
Pam must have sent him up to check on me.
   "I lost the Thomas Edison Contest.
Nobody liked my Vending Dresser," I said to

him, because I didn't have anything to lose anymore. And then I reached in my pocket and pulled out the bear nose. "And I stole this so I'd have a better chance to win," I said. "It was Foster Brooks's invention."

"What's the Vending Dresser?" McQuade asked. So I told him about my boring invention that did not win, and when I finished, McQuade looked me in the eye, and he told me he would buy one if he could.

"Why?" I said.

"Because I'm not good at picking clothes," he replied. I checked out his flannel shirt. It was kind of ugly.

"Maybe you should try a new color," I said.

"If you say so," McQuade replied, "I will."

"I say so," I told him, and I couldn't help smiling just a teeny bit.

Then McQuade took the Zoo Nose out of my hand. "Now what is this, exactly? It looks like a sponge," he said, tossing it in the air.

"It is," I said back, "but it works like this." And I put the Zoo Nose on.

McQuade took it off me and put it on

himself. "I like this thing," he said. "Give it back and you'll be fine."

And when I looked at McQuade, with that dumb Zoo Nose on his face, I began to believe there was a chance he was right. Maybe I could just give it back to Foster.

"'Kay," I said, because now I felt like I could face the world somehow. The "keeper" seemed to have that effect on people.

CHAPTER EIGHTEEN

AN ORPHAN

But four days later I still had the Zoo Nose in my pocket. McQuade made me think it would be easy to give it back to Foster, but I couldn't do it. I put it in my pocket each morning, and somehow it was still in my pocket each night. And I felt like it was getting bigger—maybe because my brain was thinking about it more and more. My brain knew that I was going to have to do something with it, and I knew it belonged with Foster, but I couldn't seem to take the Zoo Nose out and give it back.

The good news was that my first Enrichment class was today—I'd never done Enrichment before. I got Frisbee Kwon Do, which was my first choice, because I thought it was something I could do with Chunky at home, once I learned how. (He loves Frisbees.) The teacher was the biggest, strongest man I'd ever seen. Tae Kwon Do is kind of like a fighting dance, and I was curious to see how the Frisbees would be used. Billy and Donnie were in my class, too. They were in the front, because they're shorter than I am. But we didn't even get to the Frisbees that first day—all we did was learn to put one leg forward and swoosh with our arm.

After Enrichment, Mummy was supposed

to pick me up. But, one by one, everybody I knew started to disappear. Where was she?

Donnie and Billy's mom came to pick them up, and she asked me if I needed a ride. I almost wanted to take it, but Mummy would be worried if she couldn't find me. I really thought she would show up, even if she was late. So they left, and I stayed there a little longer, but as I looked around, more and more kids kept leaving. There weren't that many there anymore. I was beginning to get concerned. I couldn't walk home by myself. It was too far. And I had reminded Mummy that Enrichment started today—I didn't really think she'd leave me to fend for myself. But as a few more kids began to go home, I decided to leave, too. It would be terrible to be the last person left in the cafeteria.

I didn't want anybody to know that my mother forgot me. And so I went to wait outside the school. I squinted my eyes up the road to see if a green minivan was approaching.

That's where Foster Brooks found me. Standing, by myself, in the back of the school. Standing, at the edge of the parking lot, the same parking lot Mrs. Howdy Doody had trouble parking in. And he said, "Are you okay?"

And I looked at him, and all I could do was slowly shake my head because I wasn't okay. My parents had deserted me. And that's when Foster Brooks, the same one whose Zoo Nose was sitting in my pocket, whispered to me, "Would you like to come to my house?" And I had never heard his voice sound so nice. That's how I knew he meant it. It was clear to me that there wasn't going to be a green minivan coming down the road any time soon, and so I said yes.

"Did your parents forget you?" he said. I nodded. Because when you really need a Kleenex and somebody asks you a question that makes your heart sad, your voice goes away. Foster Brooks took my backpack off my

shoulders and put it over his own shoulder, even though he already had one on his back.

Sometimes people can surprise you like that. And even though I knew he had told Sharon that her Doll-Clothes Washer made him dizzy, he wasn't being funny right now. He was being a gentleman.

CHAPTER NINETEEN

FOSTER'S HOUSE

Foster's house was not far away. And when we walked in the door, even though his mother had never met me, she said, "You look like you need a snack." I didn't expect somebody to say that to me today, and a couple tears rolled out. Mrs. Brooks put a plate of peanut-butter cookies on the table, and she gave us each a glass of milk.

"Eat up," she said. And I didn't expect anybody to give me cookies and say that to me today, either, and a few more tears came down. Then she handed me a kitchen towel to wipe my eyes, and she said, "I'll call your parents and tell them where you are, and then we'll make you feel better." I looked up at her, and I believed her. That's when I noticed she was wearing a Team Smiley Face shirt too.

"What's Team Smiley Face?" I said, to get the attention off myself.

"My dad's a dentist," said Foster. "That's why we always wear these shirts." He gave me a gigantic grin, and it made me smile back. Sometimes smiles work that way.

"Would you like a T-shirt?" said Mrs. Brooks. I didn't feel like wearing a Team Smiley Face shirt, but I said yes, just because she was so nice. Then she called Mummy, and I heard her say, "It happens to the best of us." I was guessing she meant that Mummy was one of the "best," which wasn't true. She didn't know Mummy the way I do. Mrs. Brooks hung up the phone and told me she hoped I would stay for a little while.

Sometimes you tell somebody a lot about yourself when they are being kind. "I stole your Zoo Nose," I said to Foster. "I've had it in my pocket all this time."

"I know," he said. "I saw you."

"You did?"

"Yup," Foster said. "But I wasn't playing fair."

"Me, either," I said, and as soon as the words came out, I felt like I was unzipping my skin. That's when I understood that sometimes, when you're honest with somebody, they're honest back.

"You guys are two peas in a pod," said Mrs. Brooks. And Foster took the Zoo Nose and put it on again.

"I like making people laugh," he said, and

his face turned pink. I knew then that sometimes people make jokes to cover up how shy they are. I remembered how he had looked on his first day at our school, how his face had turned red and he wouldn't talk. . . . I began to think that Foster Brooks and I were going to be friends. It seemed like he might be a "keeper" too.

CHAPTER TWENTY

AS SOFT AS WHIPPED CREAM

Mrs. Brooks drove me home a short while later, and Mummy and Daddy were waiting for me. They tried to hug me, but my body wouldn't move. My body knew they were just pretending to love me in front of Mrs. Brooks.

"You don't love me," I said, and I went up to my room. And when I saw Chunky's worried eyes, the crysies came on so hard I was afraid my neighbors would hear me. Chunky must have been wondering where I was all afternoon.

When Mummy came upstairs, all the crying had made me as soft as whipped cream, and Mummy scooped me into her arms. After a while I felt a little drop on my wrist, and it hadn't come from one of my own eyes. The drop had come from Mummy.

"I love you so much," she said softly. And that kept the crysies going good because I wanted to believe her. She hardly ever tells me that.

"Do you?" I said.

"I do," she said. Then I wanted to believe her even more, but I was afraid to believe her too. I didn't want to be let down again.

CHAPTER TWENTY-ONE

A DEUCE

The next evening, even though it was a Wednesday, Pam showed up. Mummy was taking me out to Fondue. Just me. And when we arrived, Guston didn't take us to Table Number Twelve. He took us to one of the deuces, one of the tables for two right near the fountain. I've only ever sat at Table Number Twelve, which has a mirror view of the fountain. But tonight our table was Number Two.

Mummy and I sat down right across from each other. And her eyes looked wider than

I'd ever seen them. I saw that she was worried . . . about me. And I know that worry
sometimes means the same thing as love. I
learned that from Chunky. Nobody worries
about something they don't care about.

Then Gaby came out to take our order,
and Mummy said to her, "Tonight we're
having dessert first." And even though I was
feeling pretty small, my mouth went into a
happy circle, because we never get dessert first
at Fondue. Gaby disappeared, and returned
with a big bowl of ridged chips. Those were
from Dom, our pastry chef, who knows I
love chips dipped in chocolate. I looked at
the little sheet inside the menu, and it said
Milk Chocolate Madness—that was tonight's

flavor. Mummy knows that's my favorite kind. She must have requested it just for me. It's not as fancy as some of our other dessert fondues—it's just plain delicious.

And then Gaby brought back a little plate, and it was full of my favorite things to dip in fondue: homemade graham crackers, strawberry hats, and cookie braids. I felt kind of embarrassed, because it seemed like the crysies might come on *again*. I took a deep breath and held them in. Mummy and I took our trip to the tower, and we filled our bowls to the top with Milk Chocolate Madness.

When we sat back down, she took my hands. "I need to tell you something," she said. "It's something I thought you knew all along."

I looked back at her, but I didn't try to guess what she was going to say. Whatever it was, I wanted to hear it with full ears, because it seemed like it was very important.

"Sometimes Charlie and the Beasties get all the attention," she said.

"Not sometimes," I said. "All the time."

"Fair enough," said Mummy. "It can be hard to run a restaurant and be a perfect Mummy at the same time." She began to knead my hands like bread dough. "But it's important that you hear me right now."

"Okay," I said.

"You came first," she said. "And we loved you so much that we wanted to have more children." She moved her head in closer to mine and said, "That's something you can hold in your heart forever."

And I couldn't look back at her. I just held her hands a little bit tighter. Because it all added up. And even though my parents have lots of things to do, I guess underneath it all I know that when I really need them, they always show up. When I really, really need them, they find me.

Then Daddy came out from the kitchen, and he pulled up a chair beside me.

"I love you, dude," he said. And I had the feeling that my face might be turning red, so I kept my eyes forward and gave Dad an elbow nudge.

"I love you, too," I said, and then I whispered, "dude." I looked at them both and said, "But I'll never get to have a big sister like Charlie and the Beasties do."

"And you know what?" said Mummy. "They'll never get to be first." I hadn't thought about that before. And that reminded me of yesterday when I was listening to Mummy, and I thought about how much I wanted to believe her. I'd come a long way since then. Because today, with Mummy and Daddy, with Table Number Two, with the Milk Chocolate Madness Fondue, and ridged chips, and homemade graham crackers and strawberry hats and cookie braids, I *did* believe Mummy.

And right then I found a folded ridged potato chip in my bowl. I felt like that folded chip had been waiting there just for me, because I like to make wishes on folded chips, and they don't come along every day. I picked it up and put it in my mouth. And as I chewed, I made this wish—that there would be at least one hundred more times

in my future when I would feel like I did
right now. And when I finished chewing
the chip, I knocked my knuckles on the
wood table, five knocks on each hand, just
to make sure my wish would come true.

ACKNOWLEDGMENTS

To those who came first, last, and anywhere in between, lots and lots of love

The Incredible Snell Family of Tourterelle Restaurant & Inn, New Haven, Vermont

Kiley Frank, my 1,000-watt editor

The real Foster Brooks, one of my handful

Jennifer Mills Brown, who always leaves the light on

Mrs. Normana Schaaf, the best Smile Maker of them all

Mrs. Ryan (who belongs in the teaching hall of fame) and her fifth-grade class at Jefferson Elementary School, 2009–2010

Librarian Melissa Foy and her third-grade readers from East Kingston Elementary, 2008–2009

And for all those who find themselves on these pages!

These recipes make my life
a whole lot easier.
No baking required!

Dessert

NO-BAKE CHOCOLATE-PEANUT BUTTER COOKIES

2 cups sugar
4 tbsp. cocoa
1 tsp. vanilla
1 stick soft butter
½ cup milk
3/4 cup peanut butter
3 cups dry oatmeal

Mix sugar, cocoa, vanilla, butter and milk in saucepan; boil for 15 minutes. Mix in peanut butter and oatmeal. Spoon onto cookie sheet and cool. Yield: 4 dozen

Birdy Nest Candy tweet

One 12oz package chocolate chips
One 12oz package butterscotch chips
One can chow mein noodles
Jellybeans or peanuts or raisins for decorating

Melt choc + butterscotch chips over low heat.
Pour over noodles. Cover cookie sheet w/ wax
paper. Press sm. clump of mixture into nest. Place
on sheet + refrigerate. Put jellybeans in nest!

Peanut Butter Buckeyes
2 cups sifted confectioners' sugar
¼ tsp salt
¾ cup smooth peanut butter
6 oz semi-sweet chocolate chips
4 tbsp melted, unsalted butter (keep warm)
½ tsp vegetable shortening
½ tsp vanilla extract
      Line 2 baking sheets with wax paper. Beat all but
chocolate and shortening in medium bowl with spoon or
hands. Roll into 1" balls, place on baking sheet in 1
layer, freeze 15-20min. Melt chocolate and shortening
in double boiler, over low heat; stir often. Remove
from heat. Insert toothpick into each ball and dip ¾
into chocolate. Place back on baking sheet. Remove
toothpick, smooth hole, and freeze until firm. Serve at
room temp or chilled.